EMMA

by Wendy Kesselman

illustrated by Barbara Cooney

A Harper Trophy Book

HARPER & ROW, PUBLISHERS

For Ruth and Claude Salzman

EMMA
Text copyright © 1980 by Wendy Kesselman
Illustrations copyright © 1980 by Barbara Cooney Porter
Published by arrangement with Doubleday & Co., Inc.

Printed in the United States of America.
For information address Doubleday & Co., Inc., 245 Park Avenue, New York, N.Y. 10167.

Library of Congress Cataloging in Publication Data
Kesselman, Wendy Ann.
Emma.

Summary: Motivated by a birthday gift, a 72-year-old woman begins to paint.
[1. Painting—Fiction. 2. Old age—Fiction] I. Cooney, Barbara, 1917- II. Title.
PZ7.K482EM [E] 84-48783
ISBN 0-06-443077-4 (pbk.)

It was Emma's birthday.
She was seventy-two
years old.

Emma had four children,
seven grandchildren,
and fourteen great grandchildren.

Emma was happy when her family came to visit.
She baked noodle puddings and chocolate cream pies.
She put flowers everywhere.

Her family brought her lots of presents,
but they never stayed very long.

So most of the time Emma was all alone.
And sometimes she was very lonely.

The only company she had was her orange cat,
Pumpkinseed.
They sat together outside
and curled their toes in the sun.
They listened to the woodpecker
tapping at the old apple tree.

Sometimes Pumpkinseed got stuck at the top of the tree,
and Emma had to climb up and rescue him.
But Emma didn't mind.
She loved climbing trees.

She loved all kinds of simple things.

She loved to see the snow
come right up to her doorstep.

She loved to sit and dream about the little village
across the mountains where she grew up.

But when she told her family about the things she loved,
they laughed and said to each other,
“Poor Emma. She must be getting old.”

For her seventy-second birthday the family gave Emma
a painting of her little village across the mountains.

Emma hung the painting on the wall.
"It's beautiful," she said to them.
But to herself she thought,
"That's not how I remember my village at all."

Every day Emma looked at the painting and frowned.
And every day her frown grew a little deeper.

One day she made up her mind.

She went to the store and bought paints and brushes and an easel.

Then Emma sat by the window and painted her village
just the way she remembered it.

When it was finished she took the other painting
off the wall and hung hers up instead.

And every day Emma looked at her painting and smiled.

When her family came to visit,
Emma put the other painting back again.
And as soon as they left she switched it for her own.

But one day Emma forgot.

When the family was in the middle of dinner,
one of Emma's grandchildren pointed to the wall.
"Where did that painting come from?
It's not the one we gave you!"

Emma looked up. Emma looked down.
But everyone kept right on looking at the painting,
and they all kept asking,
"Yes, where did it come from?"

Finally Emma said, "Me," very softly. "*I* did it."

"*You!*" they all cried out together.

Emma hurried to hide the painting in the closet.

"Stop!" cried her family. "Don't hide it away!"
"It's beautiful! Why don't you paint another one?"

"I have," said Emma.
And she brought twenty more paintings out of the closet.

From that day Emma kept painting and she never stopped.
She painted the snow coming right up to her doorstep.

EMMA

She painted the old apple tree in blossom
with the woodpecker tapping at its branches.

EMMA

EMMA

She painted Pumpkinseed curling his toes in the sun.

EMMA
EMMA
EMMA
EMMA

And she painted her village across the mountains
over and over and over again.

Soon people began coming from everywhere
to look at Emma's paintings.
When they left she was all alone.

EMMA

But now Emma had something else.
She sat by the window every day and painted
from morning till night.
She painted hundreds of paintings.

Her paintings covered the walls.
They filled the closets.
They hung in the kitchen cupboards.

Emma was surrounded by the friends and places she loved. And she was never lonely again.